THE PRINCESS AND THE CASTLE

A.M. Luzzader

Illustrated by Anna M. Clark

Published by Knowledge Forest Press
P.O. Box 6331
Logan, UT 84341

Ebook ISBN-13: 978-1-949078-45-9
Paperback ISBN-13: 978-1-949078-44-2

Cover design by Sleepy Fox Studio, www.sleepyfoxstudio.net

Editing by Chadd VanZanten

Interior illustrations by Anna M. Clark, annamclarkart.com

The real-life Princess Olivia and Princess Juniper

CONTENTS

Chapter One

IN A FARAWAY PLACE, IN A FARAWAY TIME, THERE WAS A land called Wildflower Kingdom.

It was a very pretty place.

It was so pretty, in fact, it had been hard to choose a name for it. There were beautiful sunsets almost every evening. Wild grass grew tall and lush, and lovely streams flowed here and there. They might have named the kingdom after any of these things. Or they could have named it after all of the super-cute unicorns that galloped through the meadows all day.

And so you can understand the trouble! What would you name a kingdom that had so many beautiful sights and places and unicorns?

They finally chose the name Wildflower Kingdom

because of the many beautiful wildflowers that bloomed in the meadows of the countryside.

(Also, the name Wildflower Kingdom was easy to remember.)

At the center of Wildflower Kingdom stood a castle. It was called Wildflower Castle because it had been hard enough to come up with a name for the kingdom. No one wanted to come up with some new name for the castle. Wildflower Castle was tall and beautiful and built of white stone. Like many other castles, this one had tall towers.

At the top of each tower flew long silk flags of purple and green, which were the official colors of Wildflower Kingdom. And like many other castles, Wildflower Castle had high walls, a drawbridge, and castle guards.

But unlike many castles, Wildflower Castle had plenty of bathrooms. In a lot of the other castles, you might have to walk a long way to find a bathroom. In Wildflower Castle, there were many cute and tidy bathrooms, and they were easy to find.

Wildflower Kingdom had two princesses, Olivia and Juniper. They lived in Wildflower Castle with their parents, Queen Jennifer and King Andrew.

Princess Olivia was the older of the two sisters. She was eight years old. Her eyes were green and she had a sweet, pretty smile. Olivia loved riding unicorns and playing with foxes.

Princess Juniper was the younger sister. She was six years old. She loved climbing trees. Juniper had big blue eyes and her hair was often tied into pigtails.

Little Juniper looked up to her big sister, Olivia, and Olivia was very protective of little Juniper.

Queen Jennifer

King Andrew

Princess Olivia

Princess Juniper

One day, the princesses were playing hide-and-seek.

The sisters did not know it yet, but this game of hide-and-seek would end differently than their other games. They thought it was a regular game of hide-and-seek. It was Juniper's turn to count and Olivia's turn to hide.

"Count to 100," said Olivia.

"No, I'll count to fifty," said Juniper.

"That's not enough!" said Olivia. "You'll find me! Count to 100!"

Juniper was the younger sister, but it was well known that she was the better hide-and-seeker.

"Fine," said Juniper. "I'll count to seventy-five."

"No, count to ninety," replied Olivia.

"That's too high," said Juniper. "You could run and hide in the kingdom next door if I count to ninety."

"Then count to eighty-five," said Olivia.

"I'll count to eighty-*two*," said Juniper, "but that's it." Juniper covered her eyes and began counting to eighty-two. "One, two, three, four, five."

"Not so fast!" Olivia complained. "Count slowly!"

"Fine!" said Juniper. "Six. Seven. Eight."

"Start over!"

"Fine!" said Juniper, her eyes still covered. "One. Two. Three. Four."

Olivia hurried away and began searching the castle for somewhere good to hide.

Behind the velvet curtains in the great chamber? "No," Olivia thought, "I've hidden there too many times. It's the first place Juniper will look."

How about under a bed in one of the castle's guest rooms? "No," thought Olivia, "too dusty." (Olivia was not fond of dust.)

Could Olivia hide in one of the castle's many bathrooms? "No," she thought, "bathrooms are not great places to hide. Someone might come into the bathroom where I'm hiding, which could be very awkward!"

The kitchen and pantry were great hiding places, but Olivia thought, "No, that might upset Miss Beets, the head chef. She's in charge of all snacks and desserts, so it's best not to bother her."

Princess Olivia didn't think of hiding in the guard room or the dungeon. Those places were always full of big, burly castle guards. "If little Juniper has to go in there to find me, one of those guards might step on her and squish her like a bug." (Juniper was not fond of being squished like a bug.)

Olivia thought she might hide in the kingdom next door, but it didn't seem fair to make Juniper search outside.

"Where can I hide?" Olivia whispered to herself. "Where? *Where?* Juniper is going to find me before I even decide!"

Just then, Olivia passed by the big oak doors of the library. Wildflower Castle's library was a wondrous place. It was lined with bookshelves and books of all types.

There were books about history and mathematics and science, with ladders to reach the high shelves. There was an entire shelf for books about how to identify wildflowers. There were storybooks and picture books. As strange as it may seem, the library even had a copy of the book you're reading *right now*.

All around the library there were high-backed chairs for reading and desks for studying, each with its own reading lamp. On the walls were maps and paintings. On some of the shelves there were strange items like crystal balls and bottles full of magic potion.

"This is it!" Olivia whispered outside the doors of the library. "Juniper will never find me in there!"

She looked down the hall. Juniper was nowhere in sight--yet. Olivia must move quickly. And so she pushed the heavy doors to open them. It wasn't easy. The doors were so tall they nearly touched the high ceiling, and they were heavy. Olivia hardly weighed more than a good-sized chicken. She strained and grunted. After much effort, the doors swung open wide enough for Olivia to slip inside. However, to her surprise, the library was not empty. Her parents, King Andrew and Queen Jennifer, were there.

"Oh. Hi, Mom," said Olivia. "Hi, Dad."

They turned to Olivia. Queen Jennifer had beautiful green eyes and long, braided hair. She was wise and very brave. King Andrew had a thick beard of black hair. He was tall and was always kind.

"Hello, Olivia," said Queen Jennifer. "Come in, come in. We were just getting ready to come and find you and your sister."

It looked like her parents were getting ready to go out. The queen wore her fine traveling coat, and the king wore a heavy cloak.

"Are you going somewhere?" Olivia asked her parents.

Queen Jennifer said, "Yes. Your aunt, Duchess Melissa of Eagle Mountain, wants to visit us. We're going in the carriage to pick her up and bring her here."

Olivia grinned when she heard this. Whenever the duchess visited Wildflower Castle, she brought gifts. She held fancy tea parties. Best of all, the duchess brought stories and news from far-off kingdoms. It was always an exciting time when Duchess Melissa visited.

"How long will it take?" she asked.

"Not long," said King Andrew. "We'll be back this evening, and we'll celebrate with a great feast."

Olivia hopped up and down like a happy little chicken. "Aunt Melissa is coming! Aunt Melissa is coming!" She knew that her parents also enjoyed Duchess Melissa's visits, but they seemed worried about something.

"Is anything wrong?" Olivia asked.

"Oh, not really," said King Andrew, with a shrug. "The castle cleaning crew is on vacation, and your mother and I don't have time to tidy up around here before we fetch the duchess."

"Yes," said the queen. "I wanted to gather flowers and make the guest room pretty."

"Oh," said Olivia.

"Don't worry," said King Andrew, smiling. "The duchess will understand."

"Yes, of course," said Queen Jennifer. "But if only I had an hour or two, I could use the Magic Wand of Summerland to put the entire castle in order."

"The Magic Wand of Summerland?" Olivia asked.

"Oh, yes," said Queen Jennifer. "It's one of the magic items of our kingdom. It was a gift from my godmother. It makes cleaning up a breeze."

From a nearby shelf, the queen removed a slender box. Olivia went to see. The outside of the box was carved all over with symbols. The queen opened it.

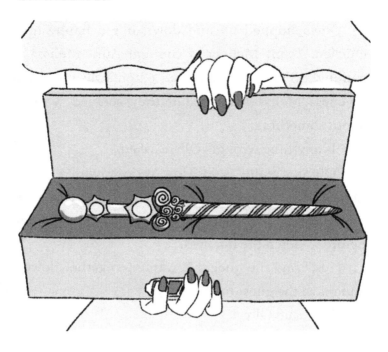

The box was lined with red velvet. Resting inside was a magical wand made of strange wood of a golden color. It sparkled in the light of the reading lamps.

"Wow," Olivia said softly. "The Magic Wand of Summerland!"

Just then, Juniper jumped into the library. "Ah ha!" she shouted. "I found you!"

"Oh!" cried Princess Olivia. "I forgot we were playing hide-and-seek!"

Chapter Two
PRINCESS IN CHARGE

"YOU FORGOT?" MOANED PRINCESS JUNIPER. "HOW could you forget we were playing hide-and-seek?"

"Mom and Dad just told me that they are leaving," said Olivia, "to go and bring Aunt Melissa here for a visit!"

Juniper smiled and clapped her hands. Everyone was glad when Duchess Melissa came to visit.

"Yipee!" cried Juniper. "When will she be here?"

"This evening," said King Andrew. "We'll have a great feast tonight to celebrate."

"I'm going to make her a welcome sign," said Juniper, and then she scurried off to her bedroom to get her markers, stickers, and glitter.

"We must go," said Queen Jennifer. She closed the

box holding the Magic Wand of Summerland.

"Wait," said Princess Olivia. "What if I used the Magic Wand of Summerland to clean up the castle while you and Dad are picking up Aunt Melissa."

King Andrew and Queen Jennifer looked at each other. "I don't know," said Queen Jennifer. "Magic sometimes works in unexpected ways. When we use magic, we must use it responsibly."

"I can do it," said Olivia. "I'll be really careful. I'll start with dusting, then polish all the windows and mirrors, and then I'll vacuum the rugs."

"She's volunteering to do chores, my dear," said King Andrew with a smile. "I don't think you should say no!"

"It's kind of you to volunteer, Olivia," said the queen, nodding. "You're becoming more responsible, aren't you?"

Olivia nodded eagerly.

"It's the magic that worries me," said her mother. "We don't often use magic for everyday jobs like house cleaning. But it would be nice to freshen up the castle for Melissa."

"Please," cried Olivia. "I'll be careful. I've always wanted to use a magic wand. I didn't know we had one!"

The queen and king looked at each other again. Then they looked at the wand. Then they looked at Princess Olivia.

"You promise to only use it for cleaning?" asked the queen. "And to be very careful and responsible?"

Again, Olivia nodded eagerly.

"You won't do something foolish, will you?" asked the queen. "Like turn your sister into a mouse?"

"Oh, no way," said Olivia.

"Very well," said Queen Jennifer, with a nervous smile. "I'll let you try."

"Your mother is counting on you," said the king. "Be careful and keep your promise."

The queen opened the box again, removed the wand, and then set the box on the shelf.

"How does it work?" asked Olivia.

"Watch," said the queen. She pointed the wand at the mantle above the fireplace in the library. Then she said, "Dust the mantle!"

All at once, everything on the mantle rose into the air. The books, pictures, and candlesticks were all gently lifted up. A flurry of sparkles passed over the mantle, and the dust vanished. The portraits and candlesticks returned to their places.

"That's easy!" cried Olivia.

"It's not difficult," said the queen, "but you must give the wand clear instructions."

"I understand," said Olivia, now with a serious look on her face.

"Dear, we're going to be late," said King Andrew.

"Right," said Queen Jennifer. "Olivia, I'm counting on you. Be careful. And if something goes wrong, ask an adult for help. Miss Beets is in the kitchen. Mr. Lucas is out in the stables brushing and feeding the unicorns. And I'm sure the others are around, too."

She handed the wand to Olivia.

"Don't worry, mom," said Olivia, staring at the wand, "I'll get everything all cleaned up!"

Chapter Three
CLEANING UP

❦

PRINCESS OLIVIA WALKED MERRILY DOWN THE MAIN hallway of the castle. It was very wide and tall, and there were many paintings and portraits on the walls. Some of the paintings were taller than Olivia, who was growing tall enough to ride unicorns by herself.

If the castle cleaning crew had been there, they would use ladders and feather dusters to carefully dust each painting and frame. It would have been very difficult for Olivia to do it that way. The ladders were very heavy, and, as you know, she was not fond of dust.

But with the Magic Wand of Summerland, Princess Olivia simply pointed the wand at the first painting and said, "Dust that painting of Lady Jessica." That was her great-great grandmother from the Kingdom of Swallows. In her painting, Lady Jessica wore a glittering tiara, a white gown, and a red sash. As soon as Olivia spoke, magical sparkles shimmered over the painting, and all the dust was gone in an instant.

"This is fun!" said Olivia. "I'm being careful and responsible, and the castle is getting cleaner and cleaner!"

Then, Olivia moved on to the painting of Duke Leroy the Third of Riverland, holding his broadsword victoriously in the air. Olivia told the wand to dust the painting.

She dusted the painting of Princesses Gretchen and Dez with their collection of cats and enormous dogs. Then came the painting of Countess Ingrid of Sugarland, who was pictured riding a horse.

"Dust, dust, dust," she said.

By the time the paintings in the castle's main hallway were all dusted, Olivia was quite enjoying herself. She hummed a happy tune as she continued through the castle's many chambers and halls, dusting the furniture, emptying the trash cans, and polishing the windows.

Now Olivia went into the great hall, a large room for gathering and relaxing. Inside there were soft sofas and comfy chairs. But it was messy. On the floor there were toys and books that the princesses had not put away. There were magazines on the side tables that the queen had been reading. On one of the sofas there sat a cereal bowl that the king had left behind.

Princess Olivia aimed the Magic Wand of Summerland into the great hall and said, "Take care of this mess!"

The toys, books, and other clutter were swept into the air. They flew away back to their rightful places.

Olivia had now finished cleaning about one half of the castle, and she began to feel hungry.

"I'll take a break now," she said to herself. "There's plenty of time to clean the rest of the castle."

She headed to the kitchen. Miss Beets, the chef of Wildflower Castle, often made snacks for the princesses. However, when Olivia got to the kitchen, she saw Miss Beets was very busy.

"She's getting ready for the great feast!" thought Olivia.

Miss Beets stirred the soup in a pot on the stove. Then she raced to her cutting board to carve up a watermelon. She turned around to pull a batch of freshly baked dinner rolls from the oven. When she had set aside the rolls, Miss Beets popped a pineapple upside-down cake into the oven. Miss Beets' kitchen helpers scurried around the kitchen, too, each one helping to make something for the feast.

Everything smelled so delicious! This made Olivia even more hungry. But she didn't want to bother Miss Beets. How would she get a snack and take a break from her castle-cleaning?

"Maybe if I use my hide-and-seek skills," Olivia thought, "I can sneak in and get a snack for myself."

Quiet as a mouse, Olivia crept forward, but as soon as she stepped into the kitchen, one of Miss Beets' helpers bumped into her and almost spilled a big dish of mango salsa.

"You don't want to come in here, Princess," said the helper. "It's like a circus!" Then the helper rushed off with the salsa.

Olivia continued across the kitchen. Just then, Miss Beets appeared as if from nowhere and almost stepped on Olivia.

"Oh, my dear Princess!" cried Miss Beets. "Shoo! Shoo! We're terribly busy here! I have no time to fix you a snack today!"

Darting past yet another kitchen helper, Olivia scrambled into the breakfast nook. It was quiet in the breakfast nook, but there was nothing to snack on. Olivia's tummy grumbled with hunger. Then she remembered the Magic Wand of Summerland. She had an idea.

Olivia climbed up onto a chair, pointed the wand at the breakfast table, and said, "Okay wand, make me a snack!"

A flock of magical sparkles flew out of the wand. In a flash, a plate of graham crackers and a sliced banana appeared. Olivia smiled. This was her favorite snack!

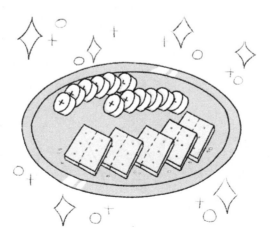

Just then, Miss Beets hurried past the breakfast nook and spotted Olivia. "Olivia!" she called. "How did you ever make yourself a snack in all this chaos?"

Olivia held up the wand. "It's the Magic Wand of Summerland. My mom let me use it to clean up the castle for Aunt Melissa, and I just found out it can make snacks, too."

"That's wonderful!" said Miss Beets, smiling.

Just then, one of the kitchen helpers cried out for help.

"Oh dear," said Miss Beets. "I better get back to my helpers and cooking."

"Miss Beets," said Olivia. "Would you like to use the wand for your cooking? I'm sure my mother wouldn't mind."

"That's very kind of you," said Miss Beets, "but I'll let you in on a little secret." She leaned close to Olivia. "I enjoy cooking," she whispered.

Olivia smiled.

"There's no way I'd let the wand have all the fun," said Miss Beets.

The kitchen helper cried out for help again, and a large pot on the stove began to boil over.

"Oh!" Miss Beets yelped. "I've got to save my truffle and wild-onion soup! Do be careful with that wand, Princess!"

Miss Beets rushed back to her cooking.

Olivia ate her snack. The graham crackers were crunchy and the banana was sweet. Even though she had promised her mother she'd use the Magic Wand of Summerland only for tidying up the castle, she gazed at the wand and wondered what else it could do.

Chapter Four
AND THEN THERE WERE TWO

OLIVIA FINISHED HER SNACK AND PATTED HER TUMMY. "Back to work," she said to herself.

She got down from the table and was planning to take her plate into the kitchen, as she always did. But the noise and clatter from the kitchen had gotten louder. She saw Miss Beets and her helpers cooking, mixing, and rushing around.

"This will be easy," said Olivia. She placed the empty plate on the table again, aimed the wand at it, and commanded, "Wand, clean this dish and put it away."

Olivia watched as the magic sparkles carried the dish to the sink, scrubbed it with soap and water, dried it with a towel, and returned it to the cupboard, all without disturbing Miss Beets or a single kitchen helper. Olivia nodded happily, but then she heard a familiar little voice behind her.

"Whoa!"

Olivia turned around and saw Princess Juniper. She had come into the breakfast nook by another way.

"How did you do that?" Juniper asked.

Olivia hid the wand behind her back. "What are you doing here?" she asked Juniper.

"I finished my welcome banner for the duchess," she said. She held up her banner. It was covered with glitter and colorful marker ink. "Now I'm hungry and want a snack. But everyone is too busy to help me."

"We'll be having a big dinner tonight," said Olivia.

"Yeah, I know," said Juniper. "I can smell it. It smells so good, that's why I want a little something to eat right now. Maybe I can use my hide-and-seek sneaking skills to slip into the kitchen."

Juniper crept toward the kitchen, but Olivia stopped her.

"No, Juniper," said Olivia. "You don't want to go in there. I almost got a dish of mango salsa spilled on my head!"

Juniper frowned. "How did you get a snack? And how did you make that plate fly away?"

"Okay," said Olivia. "Sit down, and I'll fix you a snack."

Juniper climbed into a chair and waited.

Olivia brought out the wand, pointed it at the table, and said, "Wand, make Juniper a snack!"

The sparkles swirled on the plate and a piece of buttered toast, black olives, and celery appeared on a plate. This was Juniper's favorite snack.

Juniper's eyes grew wide. "A magic wand!" she yelled.

Olivia hid it behind her back again.

"Where did you get it?" asked Juniper.

"It's Mom's," said Olivia. "She said I could use it to clean up the castle before Duchess Melissa arrives."

"Give it to me!" cried Juniper.

"No way," said Olivia. "Mom gave it to me. I'm responsible for it."

"Give it, Olivia," Juniper repeated.

"No. Eat your snack," said Olivia.

Juniper jumped out of her chair. "I don't want the snack now. I want to look at that wand!"

Olivia kept the wand behind her back.

"Olivia! Let me see it!" cried Juniper.

They began to struggle. Juniper grabbed at the wand. Olivia scurried into the kitchen with Juniper close behind her. Olivia tripped a kitchen helper carrying a cherry pie. It fell to the floor and broke into an awful mess. Juniper stepped in it and left cherry pie footprints across the floor. Then Juniper crashed into Miss Beets, who had just then opened a big can of green beans. The beans were tossed into the air and into a pan of sauce simmering on a side burner. Miss Beets tried to save the sauce, but she elbowed one of her helpers, who stumbled into the big spice rack. All the spice bottles clattered onto the floor. More helpers tripped and collided as the two princesses raced around them.

Olivia had cleaned one half of the castle, but now the kitchen was a disaster.

Chapter Five
BE CAREFUL

OLIVIA RAN THROUGH THE CASTLE HOLDING THE WAND high in the air. Juniper was close behind her with her arms outstretched. Juniper was younger and smaller than her big sister. Olivia was usually much faster than her little sister, but Juniper was doing a marvelous job of keeping up. She really wanted that wand.

"Let me see it!" cried Juniper.

"See with your eyes, not with your hands!" replied Olivia.

All through the castle, Olivia ran and Juniper chased. Olivia bumped into Duke Leroy's suit of armor, which stood quiet and handsome in one of the hallways. It teetered and then crashed to the floor with an awful racket. Olivia knocked Queen Jennifer's big potted fern off its stand, and it shattered on the carpeting. Everywhere they went, the sisters left tipped-over furniture, rumpled rugs, and broken decorations.

As you know, the princesses sometimes quarreled. They were acting more like two puppies fighting over a bone than princesses. They wrestled and tussled, and then they *wussled*, which isn't even a real word.

Finally, Olivia turned to Juniper and said, "Quit it, Juniper!" She pointed the wand at her sister. "Or I'll use this wand to turn you into a mouse!"

A strange thing happened then.

Juniper disappeared.

That's what Olivia *thought* had happened, but when she had a closer look, she learned that Juniper had *not* disappeared. Instead, Juniper had been trans-formed into a tiny little white house mouse.

For a moment, Olivia admired how cute Juniper was, with her big eyes, wiggly pink nose, and cute little whiskers. But then she came to her senses.

"No!" cried Olivia. "I didn't mean to turn you into a mouse!"

Angry squeaking noises came from Juniper the mouse, which Olivia knew meant, "Change me back *right now!*"

Olivia quickly stood and pointed the wand at her mouse-sister. "Wand," she said urgently, "change my sister back into a princess!"

But nothing happened.

Juniper hopped up and down. Then she scurried around in a little circle. None of this helped.

Olivia pointed the wand again. "Change Juniper back into a girl!"

Still nothing.

Olivia shook the wand in the air and tried again. Nothing. She tapped the wand on the palm of her hand and tried again. Nothing. No little girl appeared in place of the mouse.

"Why isn't this working?" Olivia cried.

Strange zapping noises came from the tip of the wand, along with a few small sparks, but no magic.

"*Squeak, squeak, squeak!*"

Olivia got down on all fours. "What did you say?"

The mouse hopped around angrily. "*Squeak, squeak, squeeeeak!*"

"That's what I thought you said. I don't know why it's not working! And I *can't* go ask for help. If Mom finds out that I used the wand to turn you into a mouse, she'll be very angry."

Juniper did not care. Juniper wanted to be a human girl again. She also had a sudden craving for a bit of cheese.

"*Squeak, squeak, squeak!*"

In truth, Olivia was a little bit glad that Juniper was a mouse because now she was too small to keep messing up the castle. But Olivia was also worried about her little sister, who was now even littler. She was so little, she could have been stepped on and squished, and as you know, Juniper was not fond of being squished.

Unfortunately, both girls were so distracted, they did not notice that they were being watched. From across the room, they were being secretly spied upon by someone named Henry the Eighth.

Chapter Six
HENRY THE EIGHTH

MICE WHO LIVE IN MAGIC KINGDOMS SOMETIMES DO not like their outdoor homes in grassy meadows. Some mice don't enjoy getting rained on or being cold in the winter. These mice look at the castles in magic kingdoms, and they notice that the castles have lots of cracks and crevices to live in. They notice there are lots of crumbs of food to snack on.

And so lots of mice in lots of kingdoms move into the castles.

It's a fact. Many mice live in castles. And you probably know what the people in the castles do about this. They keep lots of cats around. It's a common tradition. Castles have cats to keep away mice.

This was not so at Wildflower Castle.

At Wildflower Castle, there were no cracks for mice to creep into. Wildflower Castle had no holes for mice to live in. And Miss Beets kept the kitchen so tidy, there were few crumbs of food for mice to snack on. The mice of Wildflower Kingdom remained in their meadows.

And so, because there were no mice in Wildflower Castle, the queen and king did not keep lots of cats around to chase mice away. There was only one cat who lived in Wildflower Castle.

His name was Henry the Eighth.

Everyone in the castle loved Henry. He was big and fluffy and his fur was nice to pet.

But Henry was bored. He was a cat with no mice to catch. He spent most of his time sleeping on the numerous beds in the castle. When he wasn't sleeping, he sat on a window sill and thought about sleeping. Henry also did quite a bit of stretching and yawning. Now and then he'd play with a ball of yarn, or drink a saucer of milk, or go for a walk and swat at a butterfly. But these things made him sleepy, and so he'd go find a bed or chair to sleep on again.

The one thing Henry the Eighth had always wanted to do was catch a mouse. Henry liked napping and chasing butterflies. And he liked sipping saucers of milk. There was a nice man in the castle named Lucas who took care of all the animals. Lucas gave Henry milk, and he even made a special blend of cat food. It was delicious.

But Henry the Eighth knew that cats who lived in other castles had great fun eating mice. Henry's uncle, a cat named Edward the Fifth, was a legendary mouse hunter. And Henry's own mother, a fine furry kitty named Queen Elizabeth, had taught Henry the fine feline arts of sneaking, stalking, creeping, and pouncing.

Sadly, for Henry, there was no need to sneak, stalk, creep, or pounce.

And so when Henry the Eighth spotted the little fluffy white mouse, hopping and squeaking at the other end of the room, he knew what he was going to do. He would hunt that mouse. He would sneak up on the mouse. He would stalk over to the mouse. And then, at last, he would pounce upon the mouse!

Henry began his hunt. His tail twitched as he silently stalked through the room, getting always closer to his prey. He sneaked down from the chair he'd been napping on. He crept behind some curtains. Then he went under a large chair and lurked in its shadow.

Of course, Henry the Eighth had no way of knowing that the tiny white mouse was really Juniper, the little princess who often combed his fur and took naps with him. If he'd known, Henry would have *probably* given up. We can only say "probably," however, because Henry the Eighth *was* a cat, after all, and all cats want to catch mice.

Princesses Olivia and Juniper didn't notice the cat slinking along.

Olivia paced back and forth saying, "What should I do? What should I do?"

Princess Juniper was squeaking, *"Squeak, squeak, squeak!"* which in this case probably meant *"Go get help!"* in mouse-speak. Or it could have meant, *"Don't let me get squished!"* It didn't really matter. Either way, Olivia needed to help little Juniper the mouse return to being Juniper the little girl.

Henry the Eighth was now behind a bookcase only a few paces away. He was pleased that neither the mouse nor the girl Olivia had heard him sneaking or noticed him creeping.

"I've still got it!" thought Henry the Eighth. "Just the way Mother taught me."

It was time to get the mouse. Henry the Eighth flattened his ears, narrowed his eyes, and prepared to pounce.

He stared at the mouse.

His tail twitched crazily.

Then he pounced! His sharp fangs showed and his claws were extended. He flew gracefully through the air toward the tiny, furry, juicy white mouse!

Chapter Seven
NO MICE FOR SNACKS

HENRY THE EIGHTH KNEW HE WOULD MAKE THE perfect landing. The mouse hadn't seen him coming, and soon it would be trapped in his claws.

But Henry the Eighth had been so careful in his hunting, he hadn't noticed that someone else had come into the room.

As he soared toward the little white mouse, a pair of strong hands plucked him right out of the air.Henry the Eighth yowled. Who had grabbed him just as he was ready to catch the mouse?

It was Lucas, the man who fed Henry with saucers of milk and homemade cat food. Lucas also took care of the unicorns and the unicorn stable.

He brushed the unicorns after they went riding, and sometimes he would braid their tails and manes. If Olivia or Juniper asked nicely, he would even add in ribbons and flowers. Lucas loved all animals, which made him particularly good at his job.

"Silly cat," said Lucas, holding Henry the Eighth in his arms like a big furry baby.

Henry yowled again and squirmed.

"You wouldn't want to eat *that* mouse!" scolded Lucas. "That mouse is Princess Juniper!"

When Olivia heard Lucas's voice, she turned around and realized what had almost happened. She picked up the little mouse that used to be her sister. You'll remember that even when the sisters were fighting, they were still best friends. Olivia was very protective of her little sister, even though it was she who turned her into a mouse.

"Hello, Mr. Lucas," said Olivia.

"Squeeeak," squeaked Juniper the mouse.

"Well hello, princesses," said Lucas with a smile.

Henry the Eighth seemed to realize his mistake. But he was still very disappointed. "Will I never get to catch a mouse?" he thought. He finally wiggled out of Lucas's grasp and disappeared, off to take another much-needed nap.

Lucas gently took Juniper the mouse by the tail and said, "I thought this little mouse looked familiar. How did this happen?"

"Oh, Mr. Lucas! It's all a terrible mistake! I accidentally turned Juniper into a mouse using this magic wand!" Olivia showed him the Magic Wand of Summerland.

Lucas frowned. "And Juniper the mouse was almost Henry the Eighth's pre-dinner snack."

"I know!" said Olivia. "I tried to change her back, but the wand is broken!"

Lucas set Juniper gently on a table. She seemed to calm down a little now that Lucas was there. But she was now very hungry for a chunk of cheese.

"May I have a look at that wand?" said Lucas. He held out his hand.

Olivia handed the wand to him.

Lucas waved it in the air a few times and it again made the strange zapping sound. "Ah, I see what the problem is. It's out of power and needs to be charged."

"*Out of power*?" Olivia asked in disbelief.

"Yeah, magical wands must be charged up sometimes. Is this wand kept in a special box?" asked Lucas.

Olivia shook her head in excitement. "Yes! It's a fancy wooden box with carvings on the outside and velvet on the inside."

Lucas nodded. "Well, all you need to do is put the wand back in the box to restore its magical energy. Then, after a while, you can use the wand to turn your sister back into a princess."

"Oh, I'm so glad!" said Olivia.

Lucas picked up mouse Juniper again and handed her to Olivia. "You'd better keep your sister in your pocket. I think Henry the Eighth realized who she really is, but you can never tell with cats."

"Okay, I will," said Olivia. "I won't let her out of my sight!"

"Great," said Lucas. "I'll go find Henry the Eighth. Maybe if I give his fur a good brushing, he won't feel so cross."

"Thank you, Mr. Lucas," said Olivia as she hurried toward the library.

Chapter Eight
THINGS AREN'T LOOKING GOOD

OLIVIA RETURNED THE WAND TO THE BOX IN THE library. The wand hummed with magical energy. Olivia knew she would have to wait a while before it would do magic again.

"I'm so sorry, Juniper," Olivia said to her mouse sister. "I'll get you fixed as soon as I can."

Mouse Juniper wiggled her nose, which Olivia took to mean that her sister understood and had forgiven her.

But there was another problem. As Olivia had walked to the library, she had noticed the overturned fern. She saw pieces of Duke Leroy's armor scattered around. There were messes everywhere! Instead of making the castle cleaner, Olivia had made it messier.

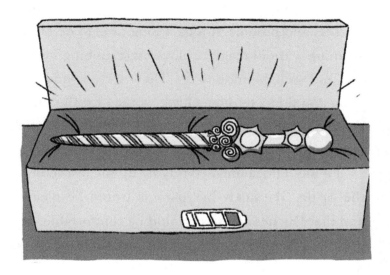

Olivia looked at a cuckoo clock in the library. There was still some time before evening, but she couldn't wait for the wand. It might be hours before it recharged.

There were only two choices. The first was to not clean up the castle and disappoint her parents and the duchess. The second was to start again and do all of the cleaning without magic.

"Juniper," she told the mouse. "I wasn't very

responsible. But I will be now, even if I don't have any magic to use."

She found dust cloths and glass cleaner and mop buckets and brooms. It took a long time to do all the cleaning without magic. There was scrubbing, sweeping, and straightening to do. There were windows to wash and floors to mop. Olivia worked for the rest of the day without stopping. Juniper stayed in Olivia's pocket, watching as her sister worked and worked.

Finally, Olivia finished tidying up the last room in the castle. She knew her parents would be pleased and that Duchess Melissa would be comfortable. She even had time to gather wildflowers for Melissa, as her mother had wanted to do. They filled the guest room with a sweet smell.

But Olivia was tired! She wished that she'd kept cleaning with the wand and not gotten into a fight with her sister. It would have been much easier that way.

Olivia pulled Juniper out of her pocket. "Well, sis, let's go see if the wand has enough magical energy to change you back."

"Squeak!" squeaked Juniper.

Chapter Nine
THE DUCHESS ARRIVES

Back in the library, Olivia retrieved the wand and set Juniper on the floor. She pointed the wand at Juniper and said, "Wand, *please*, turn my sister back into a human girl."

The wand sputtered. Then the wand sparked.

Then it made a sort of crackling noise.

And then nothing more.

"Oh no!" cried Olivia. "It needs more time to recharge! But Mom and Dad and Melissa will be here any moment!"

Just then, the wand sent out a swarm of warm sparkles, which swirled around little Juniper the mouse, and in another instant, Juniper was a girl again!

Both sisters were very glad, and they hugged one another.

"I'm sorry I turned you into a mouse," said Olivia.

"That's okay," said Juniper. "It was a little bit fun."

"It was?" asked Olivia.

"Yes," Juniper replied, "but I wouldn't want to be a mouse forever."

"I'm also sorry that I wouldn't let you look at the wand," said Olivia. "You can look at it now if you want."

Olivia held the wand out toward Juniper. But Juniper waved her hands and backed away.

"No, no, no!" Juniper cried. "I think I've had enough of the magic wand for one day! Perhaps another time."

Olivia laughed and nodded. "I know what you mean."

Just then they heard unicorns neighing happily at the front entrance.

"It's Duchess Melissa!" cried the sisters.

The princesses hurried to the breakfast nook to get the mostly finished welcome sign. Then they ran to the front entrance. Duchess Melissa climbed down from the carriage and gave both the girls great big hugs. Princess Juniper helped the duchess carry her things to the guest room. Juniper was small, but she was fairly strong for her size.

As the duchess and Juniper went to the guest room, Queen Jennifer looked around the castle in wonder.

"Olivia!" she said. "You've done very well! The castle looks beautiful! I guess I didn't need to worry about you using the wand."

Olivia frowned and poked her toe at the stony floor. "Actually," she said, "things didn't go so smoothly, Mom."

Olivia told the whole story. She told of racing through the castle and messing things up. She told of turning Juniper into a mouse. And then she explained that she'd finally cleaned things up without magic. Her parents listened closely.

"Things were going so well," groaned Olivia. "I was responsible, but then I made a few unwise choices. I'm sorry."

The queen said, "You made a mistake Olivia, but you took responsibility for your actions by admitting your mistake, fixing it, and apologizing. It seems you even came up with your own punishment, which was cleaning the castle without the help of magic."

King Andrew shook his head and said, "That's a punishment I wouldn't wish on *anyone!*"

"Everyone makes mistakes," said the queen to Olivia. "Next time you're given a responsibility, be thoughtful, remember your past mistakes, and all will be well."

Queen Jennifer gave Olivia a big hug, and Olivia was glad that her parents were not angry.

Duchess Melissa and Princess Juniper came to the great hall for the big feast that Miss Beets had prepared. First came the truffle and wild-onion soup. Next came beautiful stuffed peppers covered in a yummy cranberry and garlic sauce. They feasted on watermelon and banana salad. They feasted on so much corn-on-the-cob that their faces and fingers were covered with butter. Miss Beets' dinner rolls were also very tasty--some say they were the tastiest in all the land. The cherry pie could not be saved, of course, but finally came the pineapple upside-down cake. Miss Beets smiled and blushed as they all told her how much they loved the meal.

Melissa had gifts for the princesses. There were fancy umbrellas and folding fans painted with unicorns. She brought them hats decorated with long peacock feathers. Best of all, Melissa brought exciting news and stories of her adventures. As usual, Juniper and Olivia asked her lots of questions about the other kingdoms.

"How do they dress in the other kingdoms?"

"Do they live in castles?"

"Do they have unicorns to ride?"

When the duchess had finished her stories and answered the princesses' questions, she said, "And now I have a question for you, Juniper and Olivia."

"What is it?" said Olivia.

"I've been watching your cat, Henry the Eighth, all evening. He's sitting over there by the dining room doors. His fur has been recently brushed, and he's been given a saucer of milk and a bowl of homemade cat food. And so I ask you, why does he look so *cross?*"

All heads turned to look at Henry the Eighth. It was true. His fur was freshly brushed. His saucer was full of milk and his bowl full of food. And yet he looked very disappointed. And he seemed to be glaring at little Juniper.

Juniper and Olivia knew why. The king and queen knew why, too. They all laughed.

"Well, Duchess," said Olivia, giggling, "*That* is a funny story."

PLEASE LEAVE A REVIEW

Thank you for reading this book. We hope you enjoyed it! We would really appreciate it if you would please take a moment to review *The Princess and the Castle* on Amazon, Goodreads, or other retail sites. Thank you!

WWW.AMLUZZADER.COM

- blog
- freebies
- newsletter
- contact info

ABOUT THE AUTHOR

A.M. Luzzader is an award-winning children's author who writes chapter books and middle grade books. She specializes in writing books for preteens including *Arthur Blackwood's Scary Stories for Kids who Like Scary Stories* and *Hannah Saves the World.*

A.M. decided she wanted to write fun stories for kids when she was still a kid herself. By the time she was in fourth grade, she was already writing short stories. In fifth grade, she bought a typewriter at a garage sale to put her words into print, and in sixth grade she added illustrations.

Now that she has decided what she wants to be when she grows up, A.M. writes books for girls and boys full time. She was selected as the Writer of the Year in 2019-2020 by the League of Utah Writers.

A.M. is the mother of an 11-year-old and a 14-year-old who often inspire her stories. She lives with her husband and children in northern Utah. She is a devout cat person and avid reader.

A.M. Luzzader's books are appropriate for ages 5-12. Her chapter books are intended for kindergarten to third grade, and her middle grade books are for third grade through sixth grade. Find out more about A.M., sign up to receive her newsletter, and get special offers at her website: www.amluzzader.com.

About the Illustrator

Anna M. Clark is an artist who loves to draw, tell stories, and buy journals. She has worked as a baker, a math tutor, a security guard, an art teacher, and works now as an illustrator and artist!

She has traveled through Southeast Asia, was born on Halloween (the best holiday ever), and loves to create large chalk art murals. Anna lives with her husband in their cute apartment in Logan, Utah, with their beautiful basil plant.

Explore more of Anna M. Clark's work and her current projects at her website: annamclarkart.com.

OTHER BOOKS BY
A.M. Luzzader

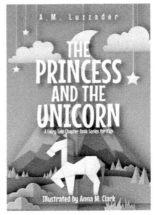

A Fairy Tale Chapter Book Series for Kids

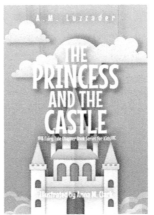

For ages
6-8

OTHER BOOKS BY
A.M. Luzzader

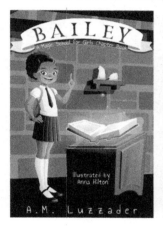

A Magic School for Girls Chapter Book

For ages
6-8

OTHER BOOKS BY
A.M. Luzzader

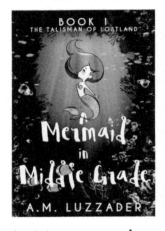

A Mermaid in Middle Grade
Books 1-3

For ages
8-12

OTHER BOOKS BY
A.M. Luzzader

A Mermaid in Middle Grade
Books 4–6

For ages
8-12

OTHER BOOKS BY
A.M. Luzzader

Hannah Saves the World
Books 1-3

For ages
8-12

OTHER BOOKS BY
A.M. Luzzader

Arthur Blackwood's Scary Stories for Kids Who Like Scary Stories

Releasing 2021-2022

For ages 8-12

OTHER BOOKS BY
A.M. Luzzader

Decker's Video Game Rescue Agency

For ages
6-10